FIRST FAIRY TALES

Jack and the Beanstalk

For Natalie - *MM*

For Archie - *PN*

**Series reading consultant: Prue Goodwin,
Reading and Language Information Centre,
University of Reading**

Orchard Books
338 Euston Road, London NW1 3BH
Orchard Books Australia
Hachette Children's Books
Level 17/207 Kent Street, Sydney, NSW 2000
This text was first published in Great Britain in the form
of a gift collection called *First Fairy Tales*,
illustrated by Selina Young, in 1994
This edition first published in Great Britain in hardback in 2002
First paperback publication 2003
Text © Margaret Mayo 2002
Illustrations © Philip Norman 2002
The rights of Margaret Mayo to be identified as the author and
Philip Norman to be identified as the illustrator have been
asserted by them in accordance with the
Copyright, Designs and Patents Act, 1988.
A CIP catalogue record for this book is available from the British Library
ISBN 1 84121 134 6 (hardback)
ISBN 1 84121 146 X (paperback)
1 3 5 7 9 10 8 6 4 2 (hardback)
7 9 10 8 (paperback)
Printed in China

FIRST FAIRY TALES

Jack and the Beanstalk

Margaret Mayo ⭐ Philip Norman

ORCHARD BOOKS

There was once a boy called Jack, who lived with his mother in a small cottage. They were poor, but they did have a cow. Her name was Milky-White.

One day, when they had no money left, Jack's mother told him to take Milky-White to market and sell her.

On the way, Jack met a man who was holding a hat in his hand.

"Where are you going?" asked the man.

"I'm going to market to sell our cow," said Jack.

"I want to sell my FIVE MAGIC BEANS," said the man. "If you plant them, they'll grow to the sky. Then you can climb up and get lots of treasure!"

"I'd like that!" said Jack. "Well," said the man, "let's swap your cow for my beans!"

So, Jack gave the cow to the man, put the beans in his pocket and ran home.

When he saw his mother, Jack said, "Look what I got for the cow – FIVE MAGIC BEANS!"

"Jack!" shouted his mother. "You didn't sell our cow for five beans?"

She was really cross. She flung the beans out of the window and sent Jack straight to bed.

In the morning, the first thing Jack saw was lots of big dangly leaves outside his window.

Behind the leaves was a great, thick beanstalk, reaching up to the sky!

Jack swung on to the beanstalk,

and he climbed

and climbed.

11

He reached the sky, stepped off,
and walked along a road until he
came to a castle.

He knocked at the door, and
a huge woman opened it.

"Please give me something
to eat," said Jack.

"My husband is a giant," said the woman, "and he eats boys for breakfast. So run away before he catches you!"

"But I'm hungry," said Jack.

So, the giant's wife asked him in and gave him some bread, cheese and a mug of milk.

But, before long, there was a…

Thump!

Thump!

Thump!

"Quick – hide!" said the giant's
wife and she pushed Jack into
the oven.

In stamped the giant, roaring,
"*Fee fi fo fum! I smell the blood of
an English man!*"

"What you smell," said his wife,
"is the twenty juicy chops I've fried
for your breakfast!"

Then off she went and the giant
ate his breakfast.

When he had finished, he took
out his money-bag and counted
his gold. Then he began to snore.

So, Jack crept out of the oven,
picked up the money-bag and
tiptoed out. He ran along the road
and climbed down the beanstalk.

When his mother saw the gold, she was pleased. Now they could buy food and new clothes.

But, after a while, Jack decided to climb the beanstalk again. He knocked at the castle door and asked the giant's wife for something to eat.

She said, "Are you the rascally boy who took my husband's money-bag?"

"Was the boy wearing new clothes like mine?" asked Jack.

"No, he wasn't," she said.

So, she asked Jack in and gave him some bread, cheese and a mug of milk.

18

When they heard the giant coming, Jack hid in the oven.

"*Fee fi fo fum! I smell the blood of an English man!*" roared the giant.

"What you smell," said his wife, "is the twenty juicy sausages I've fried for your breakfast!"

Then off she went, and the giant ate his breakfast.

When he had finished, he took
out a hen, and said, "Lay!" And
the hen laid a golden egg. Then the
giant began to snore.

So, Jack crept out of the oven,
picked up the hen and tiptoed
out. He ran along the road and
climbed down the beanstalk.

He ran home, sat the hen on the table and said, "Lay!" And the hen laid a golden egg.

His mother was *very* pleased. Now they could have gold any time they wanted.

But, after a while, Jack decided
to climb the beanstalk again.

This time he hid behind a bush,
and when the giant's wife came
out to peg her washing on the line,
he sneaked inside.

He climbed into a large bread
bin. Then the giant's wife came
back, and in stamped the giant,
roaring, "*Fee fi fo fum! I smell
the blood of an English man!*"

"Look in the oven," said his wife. "That's where the rascally boy always hides!"

But the oven was empty!

Then, off she went and the giant ate his breakfast.

When he had finished, he took
out a golden harp and said, "Sing!"
And the harp played sweet music.
Then he began to snore.

So, Jack crept out of the bread
bin and picked up the golden harp.

But the harp sang out,
"Master! Master!"
The giant woke, and he roared,
"I will catch you, rascally boy!"

Jack ran, and the giant ran after him.

Jack reached the beanstalk and he began to climb down. The giant reached the beanstalk and he climbed down.

And that giant came closer... and closer.

Jack shouted, "Mother! Quick, bring an axe!"

His mother came running with an axe. Jack jumped to the ground. He picked up the axe and chopped through the beanstalk – and the giant came tumbling down.

And that was the end of him!

From then on, Jack and his mother had everything they needed. If they wanted money, they said, "Lay!" and the hen gave them a golden egg.

If they were tired or sad, they said, "Sing!" and the golden harp played sweet music.

And they had all this because Jack swapped their cow, Milky-White, for FIVE MAGIC BEANS!

FIRST FAIRY TALES
by Margaret Mayo
Illustrated by Philip Norman

Enjoy a little more magic with these First Fairy Tales:

❏ Cinderella	1 84121 150 8	£3.99
❏ Hansel and Gretel	1 84121 148 6	£3.99
❏ Jack and the Beanstalk	1 84121 146 X	£3.99
❏ Sleeping Beauty	1 84121 144 3	£3.99
❏ Rumpelstiltskin	1 84121 152 4	£3.99
❏ Snow White	1 84121 154 0	£3.99

Colour Crackers
by Rose Impey
Illustrated by Shoo Rayner

Have you read any Colour Crackers?

❏ A Birthday for Bluebell	1 84121 228 8	£3.99
❏ Hot Dog Harris	1 84121 232 6	£3.99
❏ Tiny Tim	1 84121 240 7	£3.99
❏ Too Many Babies	1 84121 242 3	£3.99

and many other titles.

First Fairy Tales and Colour Crackers are available from all good
bookshops, or can be ordered direct from the publisher:
Orchard Books, PO BOX 29, Douglas IM99 1BQ
Credit card orders please telephone 01624 836000
or fax 01624 837033
or e-mail: bookshop@enterprise.net for details.

To order please quote title, author and ISBN
and your full name and address.
Cheques and postal orders should be
made payable to 'Bookpost plc'.
Postage and packing is FREE within the UK
(overseas customers should add £1.00 per book).

Prices and availability are subject to change.